Operation Outreach - USA

"I pledge to be kind to people, animals, and the environment."

Signed_____

Sponsored by

**Joseph Perini
Memorial Foundation**

73 Mt. Wayte Avenue
Framingham, MA 01702

Not for Sadie

A True Story

Written and Illustrated by

Jane Mathews

Published by Storytellers Ink
Seattle, Washington

ISBN 1-880812-05-3

Printed in the United States of America

Dedicated with appreciation to

James M. Johnson Jr. D.V.M.

James P. Wylie D.V.M.

There lives a small cat by the name of Sadie.

Sadie is mostly a white cat.

However, she does have a few spots that one will notice.

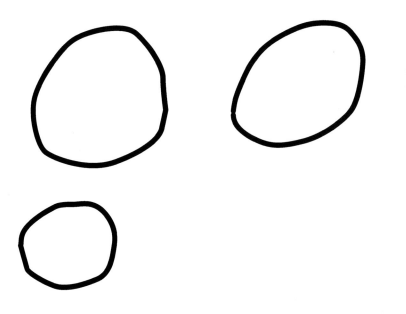

One spot is black.

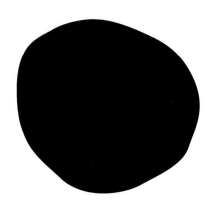

One spot is brown.

And one spot appears to be orange.

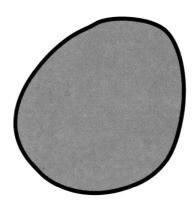

Sadie's eyes are green.

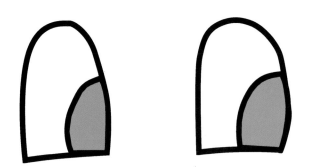

Her ears are pink.

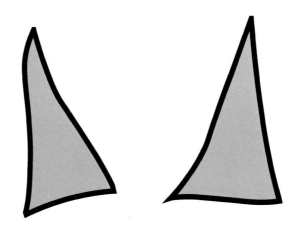

Sadie likes to jump up.

Sadie also likes to jump down.

She has a marvelous tail
that appears to be too
large.

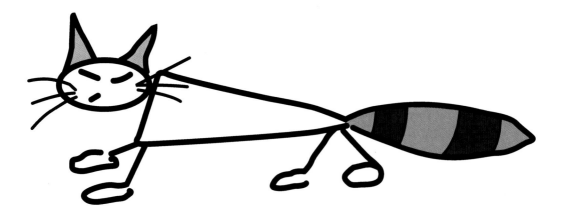

Sadie lives in a house
that she loves very much.

Most of the time Sadie is
a very sweet cat.

But at other times she is
a naughty cat and makes
hissing sounds with her
mouth.

One winter day Sadie was alone in her house!

alone

She was not feeling well.

When her mistress came home, Sadie did not appear at the door.

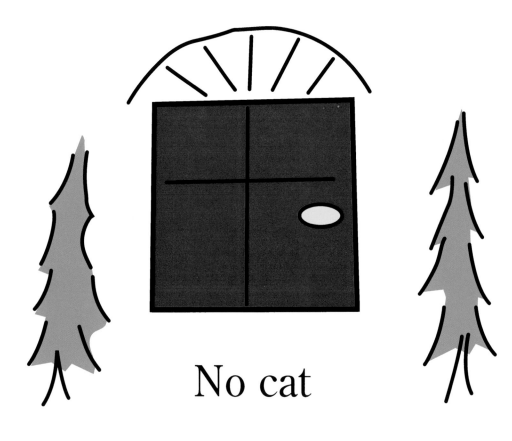

No cat

The girl was apprehensive so she called,

"Sāy dēē."

She heard no "meow" from the small cat.

And so the girl went looking for Sadie.

"Oh no!" There she was on the bed very sick.

Perhaps she has a bad cold. "Let us go to the veterinarian," thought the girl.

And so they went out into the rain and trudged to the doctor.

Sadie cried.

Soon the doctor gave her
a big shot and some pills
to take home.

Time went by, and Sadie remained under the bed hiding, for she felt quite ill.

The girl was worried, for Sadie refused to eat.

"What will I do?" she wondered.

It had been seven days and nights.

Monday

2

Tuesday

3

Wednesday

4

Thursday

5

Friday

6

Saturday

7

Sunday

The girl's mother came to visit. They went to a restaurant to eat, and the mother ordered fish. Salmon. Pink.

"I will take the salmon home and trick Sadie into eating. Cats love fish," she said.

As she placed the salmon on the plate, she said "Here is a plate of fish, but it's not for Sadie."

The fish smelled delicious and Sadie's nose noticed it right away!

Her tail twitched. She came out.

"Yum Yum" said the mother. "Such good fish, but it is not for Sadie."

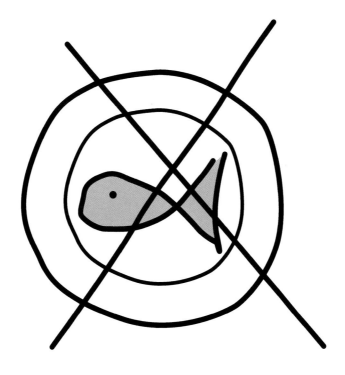

The cat's nose was most excited.

"Oh yes! I wish to eat right now."

And so the mother and
the girl knew that Sadie
would eat up the fish and
would soon be strong
and well again!

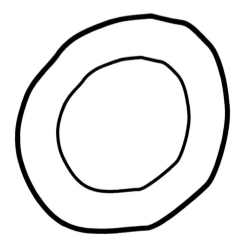

And she was.

"Meow"